**Diplodocus** is pronounced: dip-lo-**doh**-cus *or* di-**plod**-i-cus

**To Toby Aitchison KW**

Text copyright © Karen Wallace 2004
Illustrations copyright © Mike Bostock 2004

Designer: Sarah Borny

Consultant: Dr Angela Milner, Head of Fossil Vertebrates Division,
Department of Palaeontology, The Natural History Museum, London

Published in Great Britain in 2004
by Hodder Children's Books
This paperback edition published in 2005

A catalogue record for this book is available from the British Library.

ISBN 0 340 89391 5
Printed and bound in Hong Kong

Hodder Children's Books
A division of Hodder Headline Limited
338 Euston Road, London NW1 3BH

# I am a Diplodocus

Written by **Karen Wallace**

Illustrated by **Mike Bostock**

𝒉

*Hodder*
*Children's*
*Books*

A division of Hodder Headline Limited

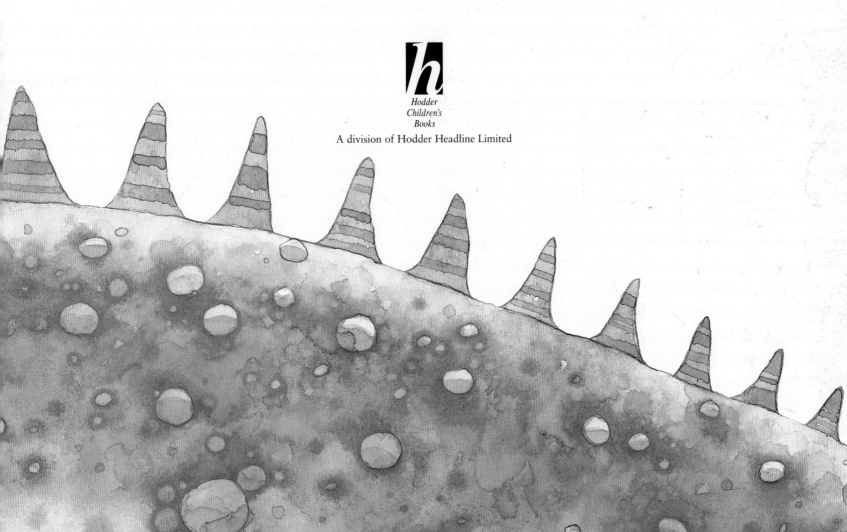

# I am a Diplodocus.

I am standing by a riverbank.

Look through my eyes and see what I see.

A young Diplodocus
slurps scummy water.
The herd stands around her.
They are older and bigger.
Their backs look like bridges
on legs like rock towers.

**A** dripping
Diplodocus clambers
out of the water.
Toes with sharp claws
grip the slippery mud.
She heaves herself up
to the forest around her.
Green ferns like pineapples
grow in the shade.

# A huge Diplodocus

stands outside the forest. She's hungry. She smells food but she can't squeeze through the trees. She stretches her neck and shoves her snout forward.

**A** hungry Diplodocus has front teeth like blunt pencils.
She snaps ferns from the forest.
She tears leaves from their branches.

she gulps everything whole.

**A** wide shallow
lake glitters
turquoise and green.

Turtles rest
in the reed banks.
Tadpoles wriggle in the sunshine.
A giant Diplodocus swims
to the shore.

# Careless Diplodocus!

She wanders off on her own.

She leans back on her tail.

She stretches up to the leaf tops.

She doesn't see an Allosaurus who stands by a tree trunk.

# The Allosaurus attacks.

His teeth plunge like knives.
The Diplodocus's skin
turns ragged and red.
The Allosaurus
bites deeper.

His claws grip her belly.
A frightened Diplodocus
roars to the herd.

Another Diplodocus
swings his rump sideways.
His bony tail snaps like
a whip through the air.
The Allosaurus falls back.
His eyes sting like fire.

A full-grown Diplodocus
lays her eggs as she walks.
They fall with her footsteps.
Some are crushed.
Some are eaten.
Some will hatch in the summer.

# Years pass.

A weary Diplodocus is
a hundred years old.
New plants are growing.
Strange insects shimmer.
Hot sticky air swirls
through the plain.

# I am a Diplodocus.

I am hungry and thirsty.

The ground by the river sticks like warm glue.

I stumble into the water.
And sink in the sand.